The Adventures of
CURIOUS
the Dragonfly™

Dear Kate,
May you always
remember
where to find
your treasure!
♡
Stephanie

Search for Good Feelings

Story by
Stephanie Fox

Illustrations by
John Scott

Acknowledgements

Publication of this book
has been made possible
through the generous support
of the following individuals:

Curious is at home, feeling the treasure within.
And this, my friends, is where the story begins...

Curious is happy, content, not a care in the world!
What could go wrong, well haven't you heard?

Sometimes it can seem
like the treasure inside...

...has been taken away on a far away ride.

7

So we go on a search trying to get it again...

...and sometimes we go searching...

...amongst our friends.

We feel happy with them,
until we don't.

Because sometimes you will
and sometimes you won't!

The reason for this
is quite simple and clear.

All feelings come from within,
are you following me dear?

But poor Curious thinks feelings come from without.

16

So on goes the search, the treasure's...

...at the beach, no doubt!

With the water so blue,
it must be true.

That the treasure we seek
can be found at the beach!

Oh woe is me what a terrible thing
To be at the beach and not feel your bling!

Alas this has happened
to our Curious friend,

Does he know it's inside?

Will his search ever end?

22

Curious recalls another place it might be,

"Aha! I've got it...

...it's with the wallabees!"

Curious loves
the monkeys and slugs
and google-eyed bugs,
the lizarards and tizards
and mop-headed mugs.

He'll be happy all day
with so many animals at play!

25

Or, he'll feel down in the dumps
Like the bubbly boo-hoo grumps.

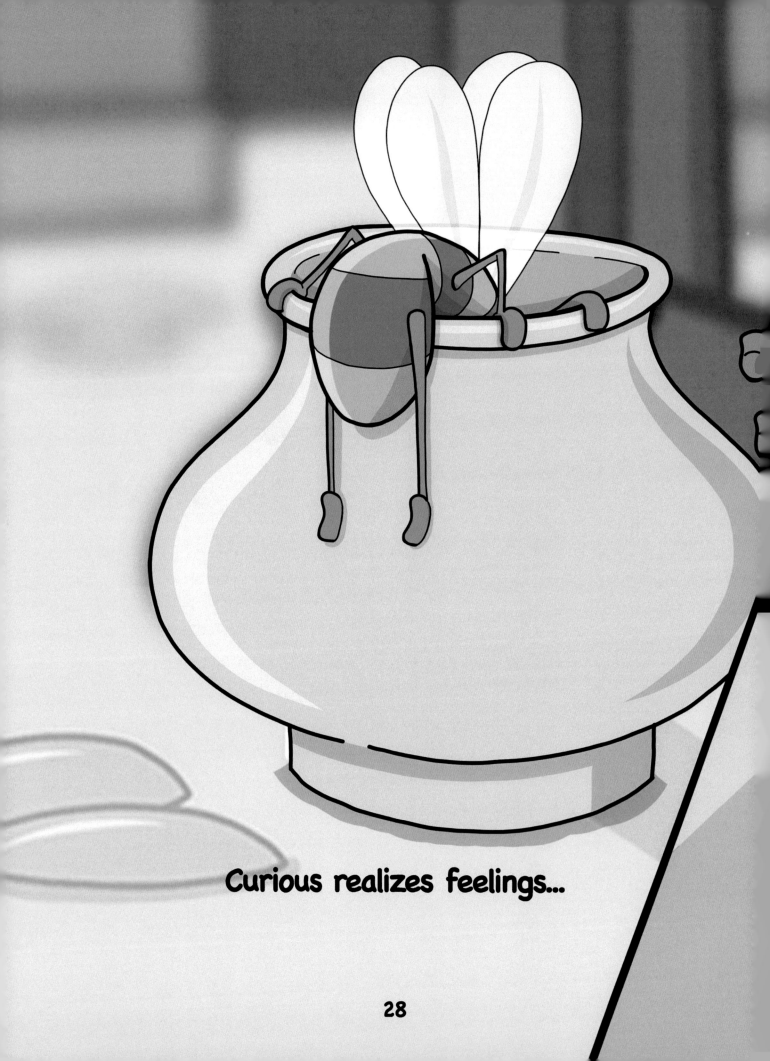

Curious realizes feelings...

...don't come from the zoo!

What a disaster, whatever shall Curious do?

"Aha!" Curious thinks, "This time I've got it!"

"I'll look for the good feeling treasure
at Ella's Market!"

"Wow! Look at this place
with all its delicious treats"

"I know I'll find good feelings
amongst all the sweets!"

"That's it, I give up.
Good feelings always disappear."

"They seem so far way,
why can't they be more near?"

35

Curious sadly walks home
with his head all a muddle.

With no good feeling
treasure to be found,
he gives his teddy a cuddle.

Relaxing at home, Curious recalls,
his search for good feelings
and all the pitfalls.

Good feelings don't come from...

39

You see my dear child, good feelings can always be found...

...deep down inside you, even if nothing is around!

So enjoy the treats, the beach, the zoo and your friends.

42

And know your search for good feelings
has come to an end.

The Adventures of

CURIOUS

the Dragonfly™

The Adventures of Curious the Dragonfly™ is an educational experience pointing children to the source of their feelings.

Curious is our fun and lovable main character. He lives in a world where it can appear that the good feelings he craves and the bad feelings he dislikes are all created by the people and circumstances around him.

Driven by his search for feelings like security, belonging, self esteem and purpose, he finds himself in many hilarious adventurous and mishaps trying to avoid bad feelings and create good ones.

In the end, he always realizes how futile this search is because what he's looking for is always to be found inside him.

Stephanie Fox is a mother, educator, and humanitarian dedicated to making the world a better place for all its creatures. She believes that knowing good feelings come from within is the missing piece of education needed to raise a generation with more empathy and love for our fellow humans, the animal kingdom and Mother Earth.

John Scott is a well-being and resilience teacher, transformative coach, illustrator and storyteller. His goal is to help people understand a fundamental truth regarding their mind, thus gaining insight into the true cause of their experience moment to moment.

We have created short animations, a comic strip, an activity booklet, and a teacher's guide through the generous support of our individual patrons and creative team of:

Mohammad Husam - Animator/Caricature artist
Sami Al Haw -Director/Writer
Christian Brattvik - Musician/Sound Engineer

If you are interested in becoming a supporter of this work, please consider becoming a patron at:

www.patreon.com/TheAdventuresofCuriousTheDragonfly

The Adventures of Curious the Dragonfly™
Search for Good Feelings

Self-published on Kindle Direct Publishing in 2019.

ISBN: 9781077907683

Made in the USA
Lexington, KY
30 November 2019